Black F⦿x Literary
M A G A Z I N E

Black Fox Literary Magazine is a print and online literary magazine published biannually.

Issue #20 Cover Art: *The End of the World #779* by Emily Rankin

ISBN: 978-1-7336240-6-0

Editor's Note

The last time I wrote the Editor's Note, we were in the middle of a global pandemic. The year was already off to a rough start, and we had not done so well the previous year (lots of personal things going on in each of our staff member's lives). The year 2020 was likely rough for just about everyone. Many of you waited a long time for this issue, or to hear back from us, and I want to thank you for being gracious. Thank you for your understanding and for sticking with us even through rough times.

   If there's anything that 2020 has taught me, it's that life is fragile and precious. I did a lot of relying on literature and writing to get me through. In fact, I'm still doing that. Putting together these issues are always stressful, but they bring a lot of joy as well. I dare say the joy outweighs the stress, which is why I can't ever let this publication go. There's nothing better than sinking into your stories and poems. They have grounded me and they have kept me whole. I hope this year will be a little brighter for each and every one of us. What I hope most, is that you're all out there writing your stories and sharing them with the world. This summer *Black Fox* celebrates ten years, let's make it a good one.

-Racquel

Meet the *BFLM* Staff:

Founding Editors:

Racquel Henry is a Trinidadian writer, editor, and writing coach with an MFA from Fairleigh Dickinson University. She is also the Editor-in-Chief at *Voyage YA Journal* and owns the writing studio, Writer's Atelier, in Maitland, FL. Racquel has been a featured author, presenter, and moderator at writing conferences and MFA residencies across the US. She is the author of the novelette, *Holiday on Park, Letter to Santa*, and *The Writer's Atelier Little Book of Writing Affirmations*. Her fiction, poetry, and nonfiction have appeared in various literary magazines and anthologies. When she's not working, you can find her watching Hallmark Christmas movies.

Pamela Harris lives in Greensboro, NC and spent seven years as a middle school counselor. Currently, she is an assistant professor in the Counselor Education Department at The University of North Carolina at Greensboro. When she's not molding the minds of future school counselors, she's writing contemporary YA fiction and middle grade. Some of her favorite authors are Ellen Hopkins, Courtney Summers, Roxane Gay, and Stephen King. You can also find her at the movie theaters every weekend or pretending to enjoy exercising. She received her MFA in creative writing from Fairleigh Dickinson University in 2012 and her PhD in Counselor Education at the College of William and Mary. Her debut novel, *When You Look Like Us* (HarperCollins) is now available.

Marquita "Quita" Hockaday lives in Williamsburg, VA. She is an adjunct professor who has never been able to shake her love of writing and reading. There is always, always a book near her. Marquita is currently enjoying writing young adult (historical and contemporary)—and most recently wrote her first middle grade novel with co-editor, Pam. Some of her favorite authors are Laurie Halse Anderson, Blake Nelson, Cormac McCarthy, and Joyce Carol Oates. Marquita graduated with an MFA in creative writing from Fairleigh Dickinson University in 2012, and completed her PhD at the College of William and Mary. She is represented by Savannah Brooks.

Managing Editor:

Elizabeth Sheets is a writer and an editorial assistant for the *Journal of Proteome Research*. She earned a MA in Narrative Studies from Arizona State University. As a student, Elizabeth developed a passion for prison education. She has taught writing classes inside local prisons and corresponds with inmate writers about their creative work. Elizabeth enjoys a wide variety of different reading material. Some of her favorite authors are Elizabeth Gilbert, John Jakes, Roxane Gay, Stephen King, Anne Rice, Brandon Mull, Aimee Bender, and J.K. Rowling. Elizabeth's fiction, nonfiction, and poetry appear in *Kalliope – A Consortium of New Voices, Black Fox Literary Magazine, Mulberry Fork Review,* and *Apeiron Review*.

Contents:

Fiction

Poetry

Cover Art

The End of the World #779 by Emily Rankin

The Bridge
By Courtney Harler
Winner of the 2020 Black Fox Writing Contest

Melanie After Dawn on Monday

It stormed last night and the gravel all gushed out the
end of our driveway. The bridge just to the left of our
property, over the gully for the overflow, is slick with mud. I
can hear the creek across the road, running high and fast.

My sister's had her driver's license for two weeks and
she still won't take me to school. I'm in middle school and
she's in high school, but whatever. Both schools are in Moth
(our county seat, as I'm told in social studies class), though the
middle school is further into town. Maybe ten minutes out of
her way. Anna can't give me ten bitty minutes of her time?
Nope. Some shitty big sister. Sorry, I mean "crappy."

Instead, I have to get up at the buttcrack of dawn and
hike down the hill and wait for the frickin' bus. (I'm trying to
stop cussing so much, by the way.) The bus winds these
country roads like it's drunk on Bud and I feel like I might
yack by the time I get to where I'm going: an old, busted-up
1929 middle school, set to be demolished once the new
school's finished. Then she'll have to take me; it'll be on her
way and too dang tempting to see me trapped in the new
middle school like a rat on a wheel.

"Tomorrow, Mels. I promise," she'd said. "I have to get to school early today for band. We're practicing the clarinet ensemble." Anna'd said "ensemble" the French way, probably to make me laugh, but I was not amused. I didn't even crack a smirk, but I did accept her excuse. What choice did I have? I believed her story, because Anna is a sucking-up, brown-nosing, teacher's-petting kind of girl, and that's a damn fact. (Oops, I mean "dang." But, "and that's a *dang* fact" doesn't quite have the same ring to it, does it? None of the substitute words—crap, butt, dang—are really working out for me, to be totally frickin' honest.) Anyway.

Anna's grades are as good as mine are bad, because somebody has to make some ruckus in our house. In fact, maybe I won't even go to school today. Maybe I'll just cross this road and walk along the creek until I get to Barber, the next tiny town over. It might take me half the day, but they have a skanky pool hall. There, I can sneak sips of beer and hang out and maybe even pop out back for a quick puff.

Won't be the first time, though I promised Anna I wouldn't, ever again. Then she'll see why I *really* needed a ride today. She'll feel guilty and I'll feel happy and I won't puke on the stinky, steamy bus ever again. Yeah, my plan might just work.

I'm standing here waiting, thinking I should disappear fast into the foggy tree line by the crazy creek, imagining the pool hall, when Anna's blue Reliant comes down the road. From the wrong direction. She'd gone in the opposite direction of Moth, and even little Barber.

The wrong frickin' way.

From the right way, toward school, another car. A small gray coupe—maybe an Accord or a Civic—but something's wrong with it, too. It's on the left side of the road. The wrong side. Anna drives the wrong way on the right side, but her right is wrong just now. I shout and wave my arms like flags at the gray coupe. Inside the coupe, a man drives with his yellow head lolling off to the right, where his entire car should be. He's sleeping—my sight starts to blur—and the left cheek of his pale face is blotch of red. I look left and right, left and right, my head an owl's in the weak morning sun, wise and slow.

Suddenly I snap to and swivel my body back to Anna's Reliant, jumping up and down, like a frickin' mad lady, but Anna does nothing but drive forward.

"Just HONK, Anna," I scream. "Just swerve. Anna. Anna! Can't you see him?"

Anna drives straight onto the overflow's bridge, right into the brown wet muck.

Her eyes focus on the coupe, dead on the coupe, not turning.

No hands honking.

"Oh, Anna," I whisper. "Oh fucking hell, Anna. Anna…"

Anna Before Midnight on Sunday

The night before the crash, I call Jim again and again. His phone rings until the machine picks up, and then I hang up, because I don't want to bother his family with my whiney voice. Jim said he would probably stop by, but he hasn't yet. I wait all night to hear his car pull up, to hear his tires crunching against the gravel. He drives a '77 Buick Regal in a burnished gold. Jim is like gold to me, but he treats me like shit. Not even like a rock, unless it is petrified shit. I know I should cut him loose, and maybe he is already trying to be the man I know him to be by letting me go in this undefined way. In a way in which he could pop back up again, ask me for the goods and get them, then leave me in his cold bed to play arcade games with his buddies. Or to score some beer and weed and take it out into the woods by the train trestle over the creek. Sometimes he just likes to be alone, and I do like that about him, but I also like to watch the train go by together. I like to kiss his neck just below his ear as the train's wind buffets us against the steep creek bank. He swats me away and pretends he doesn't like his neck kissed, but he does. I know he does, just like I know he likes me, maybe even loves me, even if he doesn't show it. If he doesn't love me, I reason, it is because he is incapable of the kind of simple love I crave. He is too self-satisfied to notice me in a way that can spark a genuine love—so he loves me in the way he can, and I take it all in: the beer, the weed, the sex in the car. Every time I sneak out to see him in the middle of the night, every time a car passes on the road, I play dead in a ditch. I fall down flat so as not to be seen by curious neighbors, and I marvel at my quick reflexes, at the way I have been able to deceive my family these six months, pretending to go to sleep early, like a good girl. I think of Mels, how openly bad she is, and I don't feel guilty. I feel so close to her, but she can never know. None of them—Mels or Jim or my parents—will ever know how close to them I feel, lying there in the ditch, lying there in my heart, lying to myself and loving myself. It's like being dead and alive all at once, like being selfish and selfless in the same instance.

I used to think about masturbating there in the ditch. About readying my body for Jim, who was waiting for me in his Regal in his dark driveway, and then fucking him hot and hard. I would take what I wanted and leave him stunned, sputtering his words, his professions of love, then race back home through the fields flanking the road, through the cut lawns of the neighbors.

But I'm too tired for all that tonight. Plus, it's pouring and likely to flood all the ditches. I'll get up early and stop by Jim's house tomorrow, before school. Even if he's been out all night, he'll be home for a shower before work, at least.

Melanie After Dawn on Monday

The cars collide. The coupe runs up under the Reliant on the bridge. Anna's car flips onto its side; its roof scrapes the guardrail at a perfect right angle to the muddy road.

Anna is dead, and I can't stop screaming.

The coupe flips upside down on a neighbor's green grass after it clears the Reliant. The Reliant smashes back into the pavement onto its four wheels. Anna's head slams into the steering wheel and then snaps back against the seat.

I watch her die.

The driver of the coupe climbs out of his car. He walks toward the Reliant and I run. I scream. "You fucker. Look what you did to my sister's fucking car. She just got that car. You fucker." I scream and scream and scream and *fuck* is my mantra, my lifeline.

I can't look at Dead Anna's car so I focus on the coupe driver. Time stops and I study him to keep myself whole. His yellow hair is matted and gross. His clothes are stained greasy. He wears a khaki uniform, some type of baggy factory jobber with a cracked plastic nametag. I know this guy. I fucking know this guy. He's Bobby's older brother, or one of them at least. There are too many Barber boys to count. I dimly recollect that the family used to be bigwigs, big enough to have a tiny town as their namesake, but now they're filthy, drunken, beaten down. I look at Marky's face, the red stain, and think of bar fights, but then I remember it's a birthmark. "Port wine," Mom calls it, which is a term too elegant to apply to any part of this piece of shit, this fucker who has killed my fucking big sister. Killed her, fucking killed her, in his sleep.

Minutes have passed but they have felt like millions of somethings other than time, like the millions of shards flecking the road, speckling the mud—like the millions of cracks splintering Anna's face. I force myself to look back at the Reliant even as I continue to call Marky every horrible name I know. I can't hold my gaze on Dead Anna so I look back to see Marky stuff his dirty hands into his dirty pockets. "Sorry," he mumbles.

"What did you say, you fucker?" I hear him, but I don't. My ears are full of cotton gunk. The sky around me is getting smaller and blacker even though the sun is rising higher and pinker.

Just then the neighbor with the green lawn, Mr. Dresker, comes out to the road. He says, "Is everyone okay? Should I call 911?"

"Does everyone look fucking okay?" I shout. I start to tremble and Mr. Dresker frowns. "Just look at my sister's fucking car," I say as I turn to look for real this time. I swing my arm and let my whole body follow, directing the two men to the Reliant, to my sister's brokenness.

My body wobbles and Mr. Dresker takes my elbow. Marky tries to help but I smack him away, saying, "What the fuck, you fucker? You dare touch me, you fucker?"

And then I hear a terrible crunching, grating sound. This new sound is worse than the explosion of the crash, worse than the silence that stuffed my ears when I first realized that Anna was dead, or as good as dead.

We all three stand and watch as the car's blue door swings open and scrapes the road. The door screeches against the pavement like it's alive, and I begin to think, "Alive, alive, alive." This word replaces my fuck, fuck, fucks as Anna tumbles heavily into the road. Then she stands.

Anna stands there, bleeding from her face.

In fact, I can hardly see her face for the blood.

"I'm alive," she says, then stumbles toward the three of us. I run to her, pushing Marky and Mr. Dresker back with my pointy elbows.

Nobody is gonna fucking touch my sister now.

I reach her and she holds my hands at my sides.

"You'll get dirty," she says.

I want to cry or laugh, or lie down or fall down, but nothing seems right to do until I turn to Marky and scream, "Look what you did to my fucking sister."

Marky flinches and falls back next to Mr. Dresker, who steps away with a jerky reflex, then puts a hand on Marky's shoulder. I see them thinking, but I just want to look at Anna Alive.

"Look what you did to my car," she howls, and the blood gushes from her nose again.

"Look what you did to my sister's fucking nose," I shout at Marky. *Fuck, fuck, fuck*, I think again. What the fuck are we going to do? Mom and Dad are both at work, and here's this wreck in the road, and fuck, fuck, fuck.

Where in the fuck is the school bus, anyway?

Mr. Dresker winces at my foul language, at Anna's face, and then hands Anna a folded white handkerchief. Anna seems hesitant but grateful—she just can't know how awful she looks.

Mr. Dresker asks again, "Should I call 911? Do you need an ambulance?"

It's then I notice that Marky is unmarked, other than his port wine stain and a shallow cut on his forearm. His uniform shirt is greasy, but not bloody, though his arm drips onto his boots. Unlike my sister, Marky is undeformed, untransformed, by the crash.

"Sorry," he mumbles again. "I don't know what happened."

"I know what happened," I say, my voice shrill and still rising. "You were fucking asleep at the wheel, you fucker."

Mr. Dresker says, "Now, now. Let's all calm down. I'll go inside and make some calls, though I don't think either of you need an ambulance. You probably should go to the doctor for a stitch or two in that nose, though. You'll both be sore as heck, but you're darn lucky otherwise. I'll just call the school to reroute the bus. Then a tow truck. Do you want the police?"

Anna says "Yes" at the same time Marky says "No."

"Well, I'll let you two decide. You, Miss Mouth, you come with me."

Again, Anna says "Yes" when I say "No."

Anna is a chorus of yesses but I won't leave her side. She ought to know that, by now.

"Anna, let's both go inside," I say. "Get you cleaned up."

"No, she shouldn't leave the scene of the accident, unless we're not calling the police?" Mr. Dresker asks.

"I guess not," Anna says. Her voice is muffled by the handkerchief she holds to her face. She turns to me and reveals her split nose. "Did it stop?" she asks, and I shake my head no. I gently push the cloth back, but she yelps and fresh blood spills from under the handkerchief, drips off her chin, and runs down her neck.

Anna After Noon on Monday

I'm on the couch, the one we moved into the dining room to convert the living room into a bedroom for Grandma, when she was dying. I see the couch through my headache, its woven fibers of russet and taupe and mustard, and think how strange it was that I was sleeping on this dirty brown couch the very night that Grandma died, the night she'd called out to me one last time and I hadn't heard her until too late. When Mom got Grandma to the doctor, something in her belly burst and then that was the end.

I stayed at the hospital to witness her last breath. Her teeth were still in a glass at home. Her last gasp was elongated and punctuated, timed to an unknown meter, maybe the one of her dying heartbeat. I was the only person in the room with her when she died, and I was her least-liked grandchild. Everyone else went home to make difficult calls, but I stayed by her body, because I could, and they couldn't.

The pretty brunette night nurse said, "Should I leave you alone, to say goodbye?"

I held my grandmother's hand in one hand while I waved the nurse away with the other. *Be gone,* I thought, *you bitch,* but also knowing that this *bitch* was going to wipe my grandmother's face and leaky privates, was planning just now to prepare Grandma for her hearse.

The physical universe will get you, I think now, recalling my father's repetitive words, *when you disobey.* What he meant to say was, "Play the whore, and you'll get death by pox," or something equally old-fashioned, but he didn't know those archaic words, just their sentiment. "Live by the sword, die by the sword," maybe. Something to that effect. You get what you get.

Yet unlike Grandma, I have hardly died. Just busted my nose. Now I have a tiny flap of nostril skin waving in the breeze from impacting the steering wheel when the car landed on all four tires again. I have short legs and have to pull my seat too close to the steering wheel, so I had smacked my face even though I was wearing a seat belt. I also have a raw, skinned patch on my left forearm, where I'd rubbed against the arm rest. I am missing several layers of dermis and I can imagine a scar forming, one that won't let up, one that will only darken in the summer sun.

I'm still on the couch when Jim arrives. He knocks hesitantly and I go to the screen door off the kitchen to let him in. He looks sheepish and smug at the same time.

And cute. Damn him.

"I heard about the accident," he says.

"So soon? Why aren't you at work?"

"Day off. Out late last night. Slept in."

"Oh. Well, thanks for coming by then."

"Can I come all the way in, for real?"

"Sure. I guess. My dad's on his way home from work. He couldn't get away until now. It seems Mr. Dresker called him and helped make the arrangements for the car."

"Totaled?" Jim asks.

I just shake my head, like I can't make up my mind, but Jim seems to understand.

"Your mom?"

"I don't think she knows yet. Melanie's upstairs. She missed the bus."

"I guess she did," Jim says.

I take Jim by the hand to the dining room couch, where I have a blanket and a pillow, a mug of tea and an icepack. I snuggle back down into a corner of the couch and Jim sits too. The dining room opens onto the kitchen. Really it's more like one conjoined food service area. Jim sits facing the kitchen door. I study his profile as he studies the door for my dad's arrival.

"That bad?" I say.

"No. It's cool," Jim says. "Wait—what?"

"My face, Jim, my face. You can't look at me."

"Nah, you're good. Might need a stitch, though."

I laugh and Jim looks at me as if I'm a goofball.

"What?" he says.

"Never mind. You just sound like Mr. Dresker, is all."

"Will your dad take you to the hospital?"

"I doubt it. We don't have family insurance with this contract job. He'll just let it go. Mom will pitch a fit, but it'll be too late by then."

"Yeah, I think there's a pretty short moratorium for professional stitching standards."

I laugh again and Jim laughs too this time. His smile is wide and his teeth are perfect. "You sound like a lawyer trying to be a doctor," I say.

Jim leans in to kiss me and I let him. My face hurts. My nose flap burns as my lips move, but I don't care. Jim's a good kisser, and I let the moment ride, long and silent, sweet and wet. I climb into Jim's lap and grind a little against him. Jim moans and clutches my ass, squeezing, until my father bursts through the kitchen door.

"Dad," I say, jumping up.

He says, "Where's Melanie?"

"Upstairs. Jim was here to check on me. He's just leaving."

"I see," my father says. He puts his hand to his side, like he wishes he had a weapon.

Jim's already halfway to the door. He nods once, skirts my father's bulk, strides away. Jim leaves without saying goodbye, to either of us. Jim's not the kind of guy to show fear, ever. I know my father doesn't like Jim much, but I also know that Jim doesn't like my father either. I should say they're about even in their mutual disregard.

My father gives me a long hard stare. He walks up to me and turns my face into the light. "You'll be okay," he says. "The car, on the other hand, is toast. We'll get a little from collateral. Guess we'll get you something older and bulkier."

"Let's talk about that later. I'll ride the bus for a while."

"Good plan," Dad says, "but what were you doing on the bridge so early this morning?"

"Mr. Dresker told you?"

"Everything. He told me everything. Your sister and her foul mouth, your bloody nose."

"Well, I had a few extra minutes, so I went up to say hey to Jim before school. I knew he'd be about to leave for work."

"Are you telling me that if it weren't for that boy, that kid, you'd not have been there?" My father's voice is rising into a shout, which is unusual for him, and therefore, scarier.

I quake a little and hedge. "Well, I guess so, Dad, but isn't that a bit illogical? More like, if it weren't for the other driver asleep at the wheel?" My father has never hit me, but he looks like he wants to right now.

"You sure about that—him sleeping?" Dad squints his eyes but lowers his voice. The glowering and baritone whispering is even worse than his shouting. I'm fucked now.

I try to defend myself. "Melanie says she saw him asleep. His head flopped. He couldn't have been awake."

"I still think…" he says, and his voice is right on the very edge of cracking into nothing. He stops talking and sighs. He takes a seat at the kitchen table and looks to the empty coffee pot.

"I know what you think, Dad, but you're wrong. Wrong about everything." He won't look at me now. I'm not a little girl anymore. I'm a slut on the loose, a bad girl with good grades.

"You'd be surprised by what I do know, Anna, and how right I am. About everything. So, what do you have to say for yourself now? Have you gotten what you deserved?"

I say nothing in my defense, because if Dad really does know everything, then everything is about to change. I turn away from Dad and get back into my wadded blankets.

My life hurts.

We are both quiet for a few moments and then Dad says, "While you're taking a break from driving, you can also take a break from seeing Jim. I want you home as much as possible. To be safe, okay?" He's grounding me, but he says it all as if I'm punishing him, hurting him.

When Dad's voice cracks, I'm a goner. I run to my room to hide my face, my ugly nose. Except I can't bear to be alone, so I go to Mels' room.

Melanie After Midnight on Monday

Anna fell asleep in my bed tonight and now she's squishing me and I can't sleep. I want to watch her face, but it's too dark. We haven't slept like this since…since we liked each other. I guess I like her well enough now, but I can't tell her so, or she'll still think of me as the baby. I hate being the goddamned baby.

Mom came home just before dinner. Dad had baked pork chops and sautéed fresh kale. It sounds bad, but it's really good with garlic. And now I have garlic burps. I might be allergic. Anna likes when I burp to the tune of "Frère Jacques," but she says I'm gross and runs away. Anna says she hates a lot of things and then runs away, but I know she's just joking, or busy, or whatever. Do I really think she's a shitty big sister? Not really. Especially not after today.

She's got this face, Anna. All sharp cheek bones and pink lips. I'm prettier, with my black eyes and long lashes, or so most people say. But Anna, she's got something in her face that makes me want to punch her for being so goddamned beautiful. Except now, her nose is wonky.

Dad refused to take Anna to the emergency room and Mom threw a fit. Eventually, Mom also threw some plates, but that's nothing new.

"But look at her fucking nose," Mom wailed.

I'm sure poor helpful Mr. Dresker is still wondering where I got my "mouth." He should have come to dinner tonight; Mom could have lectured him on the finer points of foul language.

"That's what she gets," Dad said. "She went to that boy's house, and for bad reasons."

"Dad, I hardly think…" Anna started to say, but Dad put his hands to his face, his beard, and she stopped.

We all fell silent at the table, but Mom clearly sat and stewed. Later came the plates, like misguided missiles flying from one end of the kitchen to the other end of the dining room.

Afterward, Mom went to bed.

Dad went out to milk the goats.

Anna and I cleaned up, as usual.

I wiggle around so I can see Anna's face now. The moon is full and too damn gorgeous, like Anna. "I thought you were dead," I say.

The Anna in my head, Dead Anna, says, "I know. I heard you."

"You heard me?" I ask, knowing full well Anna Alive would never do this kind of stuff. This nonsense game and make-believe talk. Not since…since we liked each other…has she played with me this way.

Dead Anna says, "I heard you tell me to swerve. I heard you say *fuck, fuck, fuck* like a nursery rhyme. Like a prayer."

"Aw, fuck, Anna, you know I don't pray."

Anna says, "You do, in your way. Just not to a god, or whatever. Maybe to yourself."

I'm not sure who's speaking anymore, Dead Anna or Anna Alive. I open my eyes. Anna is looking at me in the moonlight. She's studying my face, my hair, my long eyelashes.

"You look so good to me," Anna says.

Then her eyes close and she's asleep.

"Talking in your sleep again, Anna? Caught you," I whisper.

"No, you didn't," Anna says. "I was awake. I am awake."

"Shush, Anna. Sleep."

"Aren't you squished?" Anna asks.

"Yes," I reply.

"Good," she says, and laughs. "Want me to go?" she asks, serious now.

"No," I say, and I mean it.

Don't go, Anna, never go, Anna, I want to say.

Instead, I say, "Oh, Anna? One more thing."

"Ugh," Anna grunts. Then, "Yes?"

"When in doubt—honk."

Anna Before Dawn on Tuesday

How can I describe the feeling of imminence? Of the sharp bend of the road toward it? I see him there and I can do nothing but drive onward. I am a coward and a fool but the jarring—at least it's one thing. One thing never to be controlled, but welcomed. I begged for it to come, and it came to me with all the wonderful violence of the world.

I am blinded by the impact, by the incomprehensible noise of the metal. I can't see, except the purple smudge of Melanie.

My Melanie is here, I know, as my witness.

And now, I have to live. I have to live, for her.

The truth cannot be mistaken, just before dawn. In the dark, the pitch dark, a lie morphs with the telling. But when the blue limns the horizon, the clean sky can no longer tolerate filth. To purge the self is more excruciating, more desperate, than any other solitary human impulse.

Perhaps I did deserve to be struck so hard my innards leaked out my nose. Not the blood or the brains or the guts, but the indignity of it all. I remember the ditch, how I belonged there. I think about aggression mistaken for assertion, about folly mistaken for freedom. I am trapped.

Will I learn? I can only hope for a better day.

Who's to know what Mels might yet teach me.

Who's to predict what kind of women we'll be.

Regret
By Sarah Jane Justice
Honorable Mention, 2020 Black Fox Writing Contest

Your name was carved clear

Lies left bare in rough-scraped skin

That swears it never split

Letters lining cuts, unseen

On bones branded inkless

Blank letters still read silent

Shapeless ghosts stay stuck

Scratching white on white

Buried too clean to see

You are a scar shaped in subtext

A pain that still might open

In blood that runs unseen

Willing Suspension
By Kim Jay Rose

discarded words hang
between us, wet

clothes on line in
post-storm too-bright

light hazing leaves,
drowsing bees

crushing spring's
last flowers

paper thin under
weight, your heavy

stories crush
offer fire, you're

blazing sun,
tales stain lips

over, over, we
share secrets, hide

wounds never
dry, I think

my heart, my heart
will drown, your

climate kills me,
so close, steals

my breath, eats
what's unsaid

Merry Christmas
By DS Maolalai

it's June for Christmas
with the sun shining bright
on a tight t-shirt
next to a traffic light,
and good hair too,
twisting down the back like that,
all layered up and dyed,
like clean purple pigeon feathers
catching the wind.

and an ass swinging too;
that's Sinatra on jingle bells,
showing a sliver of ribbon
at the waistband of the jeans,
the paper of a present
left under a tree
and wrapped bad enough
that you know there's something good in there.

and she keeps looking at me
sat where I am by the bar window patio
(three beers in
and reading Frank McCourt reach Brooklyn
on my breaks from watching the girls)

and I can tell because she does it sideways
with eyes on the edge of her sunglasses
pale face as shiny as tinsel
and cheeks
as pink as a kid meeting Santa Claus.
she has eyes like Christmas lights
catching the light of the bowing sun,
ringing in the coming evening

like bells
in cold weather.

The Problem with Dating a Poet
By Sophia Thimmes

the problem

with dating a poet is

wondering if he will cross out

my words in his head as i speak them

shoot them down like birds

as they leave my mouth until

i am left with nothing

but the hardened core

of myself and no

excess

Unmute
By Maggie Wolff

He asks me to mute the commercials
because extra sounds bother him

      Mute

My mouth burns from the silence
Copper tinged taste of tongue
The coils of my mouth are cooled
It is an oven
where words patiently bake
until ready for someone else's consumption

        A commercial for bathroom cleaner plays out in
slow sheets of silence

Words unheard ache
like freezer burn scraping the ribcage ridges of the mouth
the mouth
that cathedral of sin we hide with our lips

        A commercial for acid reflux medication and we
stare at it with eyes closed

Words think they come from the mouth but first from the
confines of the throat
but before that holding place
is it the lungs
where words hide in between veiny walls of tissue
always expanding enough to collapse

Lower perhaps
all the way down to the tangled rope intestine

Words must come from there since that dark tunnel
is always twisting and moving
Words probably think that is where they come from

He nudges my arm in the absence of sound
"The Walking Dead" is back

Unmute

Ganda
By Kaitlyn San Miguel

The news report that night referred to her as Joseph, but somewhere you knew that was wrong. The channel flashed with images of a sunken-faced man with thick lips and gleaming eyes—a caricature of Jeni's high cheekbones, puckered red lips, and large brown eyes encased in bold, black paint.

Snatches of words caught your attention—*violently beaten, unknown suspects*—but ultimately none stick.

In the kitchen, your wife bustled around putting plates into cupboards, neatly arranging cutlery so that everything was in the right place. Always the right place.

"Papa," she called out to you. Her voice floated through the living room, untethered. You could barely register what she said. "Papa, any sweets before bedtime?"

"No, Mama," you wanted to tell her. "No, I don't care for anything right now."

***

You met Jeni on a rainy Thursday night two (or perhaps it was three—you never were good with details) years ago. Was it typhoon season? Perhaps. But you knew that it was Thursday and raining and nighttime. Thursday nights were karaoke nights at your boss's favorite bar, The

Americano, a large, noisy, American-themed bar that refused to sell Filipino food, not even lumpia, and was intimate in an impersonal kind of way. You could lose yourself in that bar. You often had.

Your boss had treated the entire team out to happy hour after work. He was an older, lonely sort of man who leered at secretaries and waitresses and never had much luck with any of them. You told yourself that you were going to happy hour because you pitied him. The truth was that you were going because you wanted the free San Miguel beer.

You stayed at The Americano until your boss had sung himself hoarse and you were sufficiently full of booze. It was late, but not too late that if you had come home straight away, your wife would not have gazed reproachfully at you in the morning as you bumped your way out of the house and off to work. It was raining as you walked home—the office and bar were both in relative close proximity to your house—but you found relief in the coolness it brought to your burning face. A few streets away from your house, you ducked under the awning of a closed upscale Korean restaurant for a smoke. Your wife hated that you smoked.

"Need a light, sir?"

It seemed to you that Jeni materialized out of nothingness. You had seen people on your walk home—the city was never truly empty—but you felt you would have noticed Jeni with her shockingly red lips and skimpy dress to match. Her hair was long and dark and impossibly straight. Her eyes were huge in her sculpted face. The tops of her breasts peaked out underneath her dress, and her thin legs peaked out on the dress's other end. She held a lighter out, a small flame already burning at the end.

You accepted her offer, and soon the two of you were smoking quietly under the awning, watching the rain spatter the road. You stayed like that for several moments until Jeni began to speak.

"I was born not far from here, you know," she said. She took a long drag of her cigarette. "I know I don't look it, hanging out in the street on a rainy night like tonight. But it's true. I grew up on MacArthur Boulevard, in a pretty house with a mango tree in the back. I never really needed to look far for something sweet. The mangoes were there."

"Funny how things change."

You took her in an alley, out there in the rain and the dark. It was easy to give her the money, easy to make her bend down and grasp the wall of the building as you drove in and out of her hurriedly. She was tight, so tight—you couldn't remember a whore being that tight, no, only your wife when you broke through her on your wedding night and she stained the sheets red—and you came hard as Jeni moaned out, "Sir, sir."

You felt no regret as you buckled your belt. To your surprise, Jeni did not grow ugly after you had exploded into her. Instead, she seemed to glow.

"Thank you, sir," she said.

She was captivating.

***

In the beginning, you did not seek out Jeni. She appeared when you were drunk, and you pressed your body into hers in alleyways and once up against an empty jeepney. The actual coupling was always fast, as though if you went on too long something would splinter.

The two of you always talked at length both before and after the sex. She told you about the private Catholic schools her parents enrolled her in, the prestigious university she dropped out of after growing disillusioned with her political science classes in her second year. She described her falling out with her parents, the arguments about Catholicism and sexuality, and then the later scraping to get by. You talked about your job, how you had wanted to move to the United States but ultimately stayed in the Philippines because of your ailing mother and young brother. You confessed your resentment toward your wife, how your mother had wanted the marriage despite your lack of common interests or shared love.

You learned Jeni's mind but refused to truly learn her body. It felt safer that way. The body revealed too much too soon. It was best to release the physical pleasure quickly, to turn her around and shut your eyes and let your imagination make her whole.

***

As you began to fall in love with her, everything seemed to expand—your fear of her body, your desire for it. You grew reckless. You gave her your phone number, booked hotel rooms. The fucking lost its hurriedness but not its intensity. You still only fucked her from behind, but you allowed your hands to roam. Four months into your trysts, you went so far as to touch her pubic hair. A thrill scurried along your spine.

It was dangerous, deliciously so.

Jeni was different from any woman you had been with before.

Your wife did not ask questions, not outright. Even before Jeni, you and your wife had not touched each other in many moons. Since the children had left for university, there was no need for the two of you to prove affection in your daily interactions.

Your wife did, however, make comments in her own way. The television would be playing as the two of you silently ate dinner. An effeminate gay man would appear on a celebrity interview, and your wife would watch you watching him. A tall, thin man would don a sparkling ball gown and blonde wig on a game show, and your wife would grow stiff and change the channel. You would hear her complaining on the phone to her church friends about the *bakla* in town, how openly flamboyant they were, how they were corrupting the youth with their bright colors and their sinful ways.

You said nothing, and felt even less.

You never spoke about it with Jeni. She, in turn, never mentioned anything, either. There was no label, no background, no half-assed justification—just the two of you, whatever that meant.

Even after the news report aired, you did not define it. Naming it would make it real and reckless in a different way.

You were not that kind of man, and Jeni was not that kind of woman.

***

The first time you faced Jeni as you fucked her was the last time you would ever see her, three days before the news report of Joseph's beating was to light up your living room.

She wore a gauzy white dress that flowed just above her ankles, a dress you hadn't seen before. Her plump lips were painted a pale, girlish pink, and her eyeshadow glittered. She looked desperately young, and though it occurred to you that you weren't sure of her exact age, you did not ask. The news report would later claim that Joseph was twenty-two.

You told Jeni about your daughter winning a fellowship to conduct research on electromagnetic radiation that summer in Beijing. Your chest puffed up with pride; your daughter was bright and would probably attend graduate school someday in the States, would probably move there like you had always dreamt of in your youth. Jeni in turn told you about her older brother calling for the first time in three years. They had had a polite, tentative conversation; he invited her for *meryenda* at his house that weekend.

You wrapped your arms around her and buried your face in the crook of her neck. You both sighed happily.

When Jeni led you to the hotel bed, you stopped her from getting on all fours. She looked at you quizzically, and you smiled in response. There was something about that night—the glow of her girlishness, the hopeful excitement both of you had for the future, the warmth of familiarity the two of you shared. You were overwhelmed by the desire to see her face, to kiss that fleshy mouth as your member pierced her.

You pushed her onto her back and raised her legs to your shoulders. You pulled the white dress, which had bunched up around her waist, over her head. The moonlight from the open hotel window sashayed across her naked body.

"*Ganda,*" you called her. *Beautiful.*

And you meant it.

Orb Weaver, Late September, New Mexico
By Marisa P. Clark

Others of her kind haunt the eaves
to catch their prey, but she's cast her web low,
its bridge line thrown between two red yuccas,
and she waits, alone, to snag her feast,
her body plump, voluptuous, the size
of a Rainier cherry suspended
in silk tendrils. She catches

the woman's eye. The photograph
shows a scrap of cloud and the spider,
incandescent in a field
of endless blue. Overhead,
her legs are bundled strokes of flame
raised heavenward. Save for one lightning strike
of trapline off to the side like an afterthought,
her weaving is invisible—she hangs
from sky. To capture

the shot, the woman stretches out,
the concrete hot beneath her back,
and disregards what passersby might think.
All her life, she's found beauty
in strange places. She loves
to let it lay her down.

Selected Poems by Nancy Sarafian

Loss

Grainy oval inside a fluid sac,
single unframed photo
paper clipped to the ninth page
of a folder labeled *Before.*
This hitchhiker with DNA hair strands,
thumb up to head home.
He never made it.
Too small for a casket.

No one tells you it might not work.
You just get pregnant and have a baby.
It's always written in the one sentence
you share when the crown to rump
is a lime size swaddled in a fluid sac. It fails
when you never tell anyone
like it never happened at all.

Paper Cuts

Each self-loathing I collect
is blood-dripped embers
enough to wound a quick disappearance,
my skin over a thousand paper cuts
dipped in charcoal indents, their purpose
sketched from edge to edge,
paper is a dagger hunting
for the right angles ever
meticulously slicing
trauma, its sting the drumroll
to a brief pause.

Silk Coat Tanka

Coat blushed by silkworms
Comfort clothes my husband says
Etched scenes of boys with flowers
Collar trimmed in gold wishes
Joy means only bearing sons

A Touch of Bass and Treble
By Alan Meyrowitz

Fingers lightly finding way
along my neck and spine,
I seem a fine piano played

at times a waltz, a Viennese—
now by tease, a slight caress,
harmonies of rhapsody

melodies but prelude
to bodies tightly pressed,
reveling in symphonies
the rest of night

Leaves in the Wind
By Upasana

I shatter like a thousand leaves
From a maple tree in a thunderstorm
My pieces scatter, awander
And the cold earth holds
Pink yellow red mottled green
Shards of me
Onto its chest.
You wander in
Looking for something
And step on those multitudes
And a bright scarlet piece of me
Sticks to your shoes
Your traipse across the meadows
Carry me to the end of the world
Then unglue me from yourself
And let the wind
Carry me away.

The Elements
By Despy Boutris

Your lips: petals
of a dew-damp rose.
And your cheeks
are the rosy clouds   at sundown
as the day blushes pink
then bruises black and blue.
Your hair—leaves
like on trees in Eden,   smooth
as the creekwater that curls

in the gutter out front.
Your knees, your thighs
    your thighs   the color
of cracked earth, of the shadow
that forms between your brows.
Your skin: seaglass.
Soft against my skin. Much like
your breath: warm wind
that blows over the hillside
of my shoulder,
through   my valley spine.

Mend
By Jamie A. Grove

We're in your room, your father and I, and it's just the way you left it before. On the dresser a pile of little rocks for your "collection" and lacy leaves gathered from the sidewalk. Your bookcase, split at the corner from the weight it shouldered, is covered in stickers. That was our compromise, you could sticker the bookcase if you left my walls alone.

We are sitting in front of the bed, trusting it to hold up the weight of us. I doubt whether anything can ever hold me up again.

There's a hair's breadth of space between your dad and I, but it is a chasm. A gap. A divide. We don't speak. Between us, we're both holding a little piece. The black cotton is slack across our knees. That favorite old tattered thing of yours.

He's holding the top of it, where it always hung low and obscured your eyes, making you look mischievous. He's running the fabric between finger and thumb, rubbing it slowly. The whole of it is pilled, thin and threadbare in places. Once, it was well loved.

I am holding the hole where the seam tore apart from itself. Your favorite part. Like any good mother, I told you it needed mended before the rip got any bigger. But you loved the hole and the perfect way your thumb fit through it. So I left it. Unmended.

I'm pushing my thumb through. In and out. Just like you used to.

I keep hearing your voice. When you were five and wanted to wear this to school for the fourth day in a row. When you were twelve and I was late getting you to basketball. When you were eighteen and you said goodnight in this house for the last time.

I remember the day you got off the school bus, flushed and tickled because you'd kissed the girl you were going to marry three times. You were in kindergarten.

I remember the time you were lighting matches under the porch stairs, left a pile of their bones in the gravel. The look on your face as your father's anger washed over you. Match residue on your sleeve.

The time you wrecked your bike and we used this to sop up the blood. I was glad it was black, glad I wouldn't have to throw it out.

Your father leaves. Gone to I don't know where, but I hear the truck tear down the driveway, listen to it disappear down the street. It's occurring to me that I don't know how long I've been sitting on your floor and that maybe I should get up and wash the dishes in the sink.

But it seems like a stupid thing to do.

I hang your sweatshirt where you would have found it when you came home.

Womb
By Rimsha Kashif

Where are you from?

I want to say uterus

I want to trace my mother's belly on his hand

These were my legs

I point to his fingers

This was my head

I point to his thumb

I want to say the earth

That it split open twenty years ago and spit me out

Like bad tobacco

Every time I walk I can feel it cringe with the bitter aftertaste

You are an acquired taste

What he really means:

you are hard to swallow

I want to ask him about his mother's uterus

Does he remember the warmth

Did it feel sticky

Does he remember how she split open and spit him out

Where are you from?

I want to say home

The one I wear on my body-

a canvas

That paints my organs

With shades of melanin

I want to say:

Don't touch, it will stain your fingers

He smells like fresh paint

Where?

I point to my chest

It was given to me by my mother

I point to my eyes

They have seen the sky split open and spit out black

Like the hair on my arms

Like smoke

Like the home your mother said you spent your childhood in

I want to say woman

As in-

my grandmother peeling potatoes in the sun

As in-

the one who bagged my groceries last week

As in-

His sister

Not-

His woman

But-

A strong woman

A kind woman

A beautiful woman

Why do you cover your head woman

I want to say why

I want to say does it matter

*Where are **you** from?*

I want to ask.

TAHA
By Kate Autio

from this distance,
i can't tell the difference
between the moon
and the end of your cigarette,
but draw me the road to your doorstep,
and i will walk all night
so you can teach me how to love the sunrise.

in that early morning light,
we will learn the new maps
of each others' bodies;
all the scars and veins
that run like rivers
through our arms entwined,
the mountains and the valleys of our spines.

while the world is waking up,
i will fill my lungs
with the closeness of your skin,
and even your name
is like the exhale of the breath
I've held inside my chest for all these years.

Selected Poems by Ayanna Wimberly

Visitation

I will love
in absentia

I will sharpen my knife
against my leather strop
make it a mirror
and there my image will stay

I will love in absentia
like a specter would

Piercing caress around you
flicker on behind your eyelids
and drip the warm oil on your forehead

Modern edicts
to protect your dream
to bring down the blade

I will drown in more familiar waters
                              lucid waters

As I am now
pearls in the ground

My calcified bones
trinkets
to warm the earth

 Understand
the phantom fist beating against your chest
is trying to release something
trying to drag the carcass through the town square

with flies following close
ready to pounce on any moment
of stillness

                          You can't afford to stop now.

Graceland

I saw a hand
reaching out toward the fibrous strand
I saw
with the lenses
of mine own eyes
the lift
and then, the snap.

I turned my back on stone
or concrete
I can never remember which
though I do welcome the possibility
that it's neither

And although there is

all that generous lushness
verdant, verdant
high up
looking down

I see the hand
reaching for the strand
and have to turn away.

And the snap sends me hovering
above it all
as if there were no world below
all dominion
all cowardice

Until I'm returned to myself
to the place where a ground does exist
as does a way to smash down onto it

Where I will appear next
hangs on the will of that emerald wing
that sweeps me up
and toward the fibrous strand

And I swear I saw a hand
reach out
and place itself squarely
onto the crown of my head.

Belove

my key is in the front door
my key is in the lock
my key is warm in my hand
my warm is clandestine inside me
burrowed deep inside me

my pulsating warm is searing
bubbling the blood inside
my key is not skeleton
and my insides respond to
fever dream loving
feverish touching

my skeleton needs the warm
my insides give it
my key can feel the warm
my insides are giving it
and this is a door
unfamiliar to me
but I rushed here
as if it were a way
to you

I am a home
making myself a home
fashioning myself a skeleton
key
so that all can get inside
I am a home and I rushed here
as if it were a way
through?

La Fiesta
By Dorsía Smith Silva

For abuela's 85th birthday, on a pleasant
June Sunday, I make the arepas by fanned
out hands: I add the corn flour, water, salt,
and oil, and stir, until the mixture takes on
the compass to whistle ready: I make the slips
of circles thin and press them rib-flat

like the 99 cent starchy cotton undershirts
of abuelo and then I drop them
into the pan blooming between hot
and hotter, until they erupt to resemble
the bulbs of barley on the chain-link hillocks
nearby. The feathered scent of warm dough

oozes out of the kitchen like 360°
applause and bloats the concave
cyan chairs and warm-dusts the herringboned floors.
"¿Están listas?"
"Sí, venga."
My abuela approaches like an urgent wind

that rises and falls, but refuses to snap back, rocking
over the pan like a steady rope swing. So glad to
have a heavy mouthful, she bites deeper
into the flaky entrails, until she wipes her hands on her
checkered chiffon dress, leaving grease stains stamped
sideways and crumbs that trace and retrace the threads.

Selected Poems by Frankie A. Soto

The intricacies of discovering romance

When I first learned how a woman's body responded
to my hands, I thought romance was heart thumping.
Horseshoes on a track—kicking Kentucky derby dirt
up in the air.

suns bursting onto a pale skyline after a first
kiss. wasn't forewarned that not all mornings
are as inviting as nights with tequila tongues

My body was a Plymouth rock—hers a moon
I landed on with flags &
heavy breath. I learned the body can submit
to touch and still not be conquered.

thrusts were the 3:31 mark of a salsa song
that never quite finishes. I thought naked
was art I'd hang on the walls—this flesh
a home she could always return to.

My palms never quite big enough to hug her
to stay before she got dressed. Never quite large
enough to convince forever to stay after the
adrenaline died down—blood a calm sea
after a raging storm.

She confidently waved
—the way you do when you know you will
never meet again. I buckled my belt back up
slowly, hopeful this delay would
make her realize my body is built for permanent
residency.

I wiped the sweat off my forehead. leaned over to
kiss hers—desperate to admit that if her skin
could talk, it would be my favorite voice.

Her index finger, a pause button on my lips
—silenced my tongue
before it became a confessional.

Sweety make sure not to confuse good sex with love.

Anger at the Carnival

The largest Ferris wheel in the world stands at 550 Ft
& holds up to 1,120 passengers.

Compared to the amount of emotions that travel
        throughout the human body
                    in a single day,
    I'd say this attraction seems quite miniature.

The one time I rode a Ferris wheel
the wind thought my cart was a piñata.
                I swung back and forth
                            so violently I recited
enough Hail Mary's that I thought God
would offer me honorary Angel-ship.

I can't even remember that prayer unless
I am on the verge of dying but I remember
being told that anger was a sin—that our tongues
can be the devil's highway & I must refrain from
driving in that direction.

The first time I saw my father use his voice

like a hammer.
I saw Hell in my mother's eyes.

I remember the first time I felt that same monster
knock in my throat. My teeth became a deadbolt.
Temper can be a quick trigger so I coerced
my heart into being a safety

I am still afraid of Ferris wheels, the same way
I am afraid of anger

I have just learned to tame
        a wild fire
                with love

Magic Tricks

I was told magic is tricking the mind into
believing what you are seeing is real.

There are days I unleash the Houdini
in my smile—can guess what number card

you are thinking of & I pull all sorts of stuff
from my hat, even forgiveness.

There are also days that forgiveness is two

closed fists
        tied
        behind my back.

Eyes suddenly have cataracts & I am desperately
trying to
        guess

which hand is hiding the better day.

Invisible Hand
By Renea Di Bella

What invisible hand

forces the bend in your spine?

Like the bough of a rosebush
bent double
with a burden of blooms.

What is your burden?

What low hanging fruit
lives
and rots
where your spinal column
meets your brain stem?

Sending noxious waves of
decay
through your jaw and
across your tongue so all of the sudden you're
sayingthingstoyourselfyouwouldneversaytosomeone
you
love.

What is It?

And why can't you let It go?

Selected Poems by Lilian Caylee Wang

i want to live with dirt under my fingernails

i wish i could bloom for you
burrow deep into your soil
the phosphorescent green of your lichen
so pure, it's blinding

i wish i could look at you forever

make a home in your eyes
the color of lightning illuminating
the tallest sequoia
you've ever seen
tie together thin silver syllables
the spiderweb that holds us together

i wish i could be stronger

i break the roots
before they find their way
a forest fire
in my stomach

i wish i could unfurl in the flame
but i close my eyes
watch the ashes rain down
count the rings of each tree
meditate on the apathy of god
try to forget that there is something burning inside of me
and the only thing i feel is smoke on my lips

My Superbloom in Death Valley

i was waiting for you under water
buoyant by the side of a crater
sand and stone in my sneakers
murky moonlight in my hair

i searched for constellations
"all i need is one asterism."
but the clouds were merciless that night
greedy for the moon's gold

i could hear your voices, like lightning bolts
piercing through the warm bath around me
i couldn't remember who i was
or maybe it was
i didn't want to be anyone anymore

i wondered if whoever i am was brave
could be brave
my great-grandparents crossed the Taiwan Strait
left behind
my grandmother
with nothing
but a nanny and two baby sisters
what do i know about brave?

it has always been about nothing
today, twisting and turning the knobs
of a disobedient water faucet
at eight, my habitual dry climate nosebleeds

at thirteen, insomnia over dark circles under my eyes

it has always been nothing
that spreads steady rivulets of panic through me
invisible as the stars in Death Valley that overcast night
a man who once loved me told me i wanted
—expected—
perfection
and so he couldn't love me anymore

my great-grandparents spent their lives in Taipei
with them, their perfect sons
in the ashes of the Revolution, my grandmother
found herself alone
separated from her family for sixty years
what do i know about forgiveness?

i am trying to stop being in two places at once
my eyes two beacons of light across the ocean
searching for shapes in the fog
i am trying not to look for exit signs or escape routes
not to walk the plank, board the boat
leave behind the only home i've ever known

but i want to be uprooted by the wind
but i want to grow my tendrils to intertwine with yours
how do you dock and free-swim at the same time?

i was waiting for you on the moon
here to drink its light before it reaches me
before it escapes me

floating in the gravity of stars i can't look away from
i have never been more full

the quartzed desert grains glisten on my palms
what you hold (onto) will only grow heavier

Familiar Song
By Nell Ovitt

I'm rolling down the stairs when the primadonna hits her high note. With each jolt of a step against my side she gets louder until I wonder what is she doing in my home and why am I rolling down these stairs. As I cascade toward the ground a bruise is pummeled harder and harder into my hip and the soprano is breathing in my ear and then it's Evangeline, then it's my sister speaking very close to my face and her knee nudging my hipbone and I am awake.

"Maya," she says. "Maya, something's happening."

"Was that you singing?" I mumble as the dream drains back into the murky depths where it lives when it isn't using someone.

"There are sirens out there," Evangeline says. Her eyes are twin suns against the fuzzy black of the room. She's rolled herself up into a tiny ball on my bed, knees hugged to her chest, and she's prickling with curiosity, the kind that's catching, that will keep me awake the way she already is.

I sit up, let the sheets fall into my lap. She's right—it's a chorus of sirens wailing in the distance, not a singer. I look at my watch. Half past three. I reluctantly swing my bare feet to the cold linoleum floor and tread lightly toward the window. I pull the shade slightly away from the glass and peer through. *Nothing to see here*, the dark replies at once.

"It's not coming from that way," says Evangeline. She's watching me, hair tangled from sleep. She's a kicker even when she's unconscious. My hip hurts. Little sister's gone and made me old.

"Yeah, okay." I rub my eyes. Still can't quite keep them open all the way.

Evangeline is peering over my shoulder. "It's the witching hour," she says. There's a trace of eagerness in her voice, and I am reminded why, sometimes, I am afraid of my sister, afraid of her because she is afraid of nothing.

"You know, a lot of people say the witching hour is actually at midnight," I tell her, aware now of how my back is exposed to the window, to the dark beyond the glass.

Evangeline clambers off the bed. "They're wrong," she says before she darts through the door toward the stairs. I follow her slowly, padding softly down the hall although I don't know why—our parents can't possibly be sleeping through the din outside.

She's in the kitchen when I get downstairs, standing in front of the window, eclipsing the moon hanging above the trees.

"What is it?" I ask the back of her head.

She turns to me, steps away from the window frame, and points. When I take her place, I'm caught in the moon's gaze and I can't see anything at first but light and something in me goes and freezes there. The moon's almost full, and I can't look away until Evangeline nudges me a little to the right, back into shadow. My eyes settle slowly on the dark, and I gradually notice the night's layers: the closeness of the trees, the outlines of the buildings down the hill and the shops out across the river. And then I see.

A spiral of smoke stacks itself into the sky. At first I think it's catching the light from the moon, and then I see that the glow in the thick cloud comes from beneath.

"Something's burning down in town," Evangeline says. She's a little breathless. I turn to look at her. She's standing by the front door, pulling a jacket and shoes on over her pajamas.

"What are you doing?" I ask her. "You can't just go out there."

She opens the door. An urgent siren-howl rends the night, and my hairline prickles.

Evangeline gestures impatiently outside. "Maya, come on," she urges me.

I hear our parents on the stairs. The light switches on, and all four of us stare at each other, clad in pajamas and trepidation.

"What are you doing?" asks my mother. Her hairpins are askew. My father keeps blinking, like we're too bright for him.

"There's a fire in town," Evangeline says, vibrating. "Something's burning—"

"Well, there's some smoke," I cut in, trying to stanch the spread of alarm across my parents' sleepy faces. "But we don't know what it's coming from."

"Well, girls," begins my father, clumsily trudging down the last few stairs, "let's—"

"We have to go down there," insists Evangeline, determination clinging to her like a shadow.

"Okay, but Maya, you're in charge—" begins my mother, but Evangeline is already out the door and proving her wrong, and anyway, what my mother means is *Maya, if something happens to Evangeline, it will probably be unavoidable owing to her knack for attracting happenings but we will all still probably hold it a little bit against you.* I know that she means this because I will hold it against myself too, so I follow my sister outside as my parents slowly fumble for their shoes, their sweaters, their still-slumbering senses of urgency.

Evangeline is running, so I fall into a jog behind her. The air rushes against my face and it's got something in it, a dusty tang that sticks to my throat. Evangeline's hair is streaming loose behind her as she dashes down the streets ahead, and I concentrate on keeping it in view. Then I remember, in an unhelpful jolt, how I tumbled down the stairs in my dream, and I misjudge the next curb's height and catch myself ungracefully, swallowing the bitter adrenaline that surges swiftly through me as I fight for my balance. Up ahead, Evangeline runs on, never once turning to see if I'm following.

When we round the corner onto Main Street, we're greeted by a nighttime exodus: People are spilling out of their houses into the heart of the town, in varied states of sleepy disarray, wrapped in bathrobes, sweatpants, and pajamas.

There's a sameness to them too, something unsettlingly consistent in their tight-lipped nods and set jaws, the way they all face something a little farther down the road, somber moonflowers opened bravely toward a blur of light, noise, and smoke.

Evangeline slips through the crowd, and I follow with more difficulty, calling her name as if its repetition is enough to keep her close. The deeper into the throng I weave, the more tightly packed it becomes. A tall man and his wife clutch each other in my path, and it takes me too long to maneuver around them and I lose Evangeline in the sea of people and noise and there's something stinging, smarting in my eyes. How did I do it, how did I lose her so fast.

The witching hour has swallowed my sister, and I hold it against myself. Panicked, I lunge past the pajamaed onlookers, and then I reach the front of the crowd—and the source of the smoke.

***

When I was very small, I would go downtown on Saturdays and eat a peanut butter and honey sandwich on the steps of the library. When I finished the sandwich, I would wipe my sticky hands on my pants, rush inside, and assail the children's librarian with questions—about the next book I should read, about extinct animals, about what happens to the world when the people go to sleep. The old keeper of the books would speak to me like I was an experienced, informed adult and not a seven-year-old with sticky fingers.

This was before Evangeline arrived, bright and chirping like an early morning. Later, when she was a little older, I would bring her with me to the library, and I would read to her while we were nestled on the big armchair by the window. The keeper of the books often hushed Evangeline, but she would do it with a smile concealed in the corners of her mouth, maybe because my sister's earnest enthusiasm for prehistoric flora and fauna made her an irresistibly charming denizen of the toddlers' nature book section—or maybe because, even then, she had those sunlit eyes.

Our library is where there were stories and questions and places to eat my sandwiches and read with my sister. I never thought about it.

**

Now I think about it. And for a moment, I forget Evangeline. I forget the creeping soreness in my muscles, unprepared as they were to sprint into town. I forget the crowd behind me. Once again I'm held, stunned and silent, in the eye of the night.

The library is burning and smoke roils up from the flames, scrawling pale calamity into the sky. Maybe the whole cloud is one big ghost of incinerated stories. Maybe it's carrying tiny specks that are coating all our lungs, that will fall upon the earth tomorrow and fill the groundwater and the river with a poisonous mix of particulate matter and narrative. Tomorrow the anglers will be reeling in sooty, rudderless epilogues instead of salmon.

There are volunteer firemen, and a few volunteer firewomen too, and they're wrangling hoses and heavy jackets and shouting instructions and suggestions and encouragements to one another. The sirens have stopped—after all, the whole town is already standing in the street—and the crowd, hundreds deep, has fallen into a grim quiet. The only sound, besides the spray of water from the hoses and the shouts of the firefighters, is a soft crackling. If I close my eyes and take care not to inhale, I could almost believe it just comes from a fireplace, or the wind rustling through a pile of dead leaves, or maybe even, perversely, the sea.

The library is old, and it's where sticky-handed children and birdlike old book-keepers rummage through the stacks, where people whisper and forget to whisper, where the town memory is maintained in modest exhibits, dusty records, and abandoned bookmarks—ticket stubs, coupons, newspaper clippings—pressed like history's messengers between pages. The library is burning, and though our whole town now stands in the street, there's nothing to do but watch.

I blink my eyes against the smoke and the heat. I don't want the crackling sound to get stuck inside me, don't want to linger too long, exposed. I turn to push away from the scene, to run home again, and that's when I see her standing a few yards away—Evangeline. She is staring. Not at the burning building, but at the crowd. Coughing, I wade past my neighbors, toward her.

She sees me coming and smiles. "Maya," she says when I get close.

I still can't summon a sound. I just look at her, at how she's watching all of us, and I'm a little afraid of Evangeline, who is not quiet or crying, who ran the risk to be right here but now isn't even watching the blaze. She's watching our sleepy, solemn town—my sister who is not afraid.

"Maya," she says again. "Look at everyone."

I do. I look out at the tousled hair, the slippered feet, the bleary eyes. But I don't know what she wants me to see. "What about them?" I manage to whisper as I turn back to her.

She blinks at me. "Everyone came to help."

How is it that she sees it that way? "Evangeline," I say thickly, "there's nothing any of us can do. Look, the firefighters. Even they know."

She looks at the fire crews, whose efforts are flagging as the flames wave merrily from the second floor. The blaze will be extinguished eventually, I know, but the firefighters seem to recognize they've lost the race to save the building's heart. One of them, a man taking a rest by the back of his truck, holds his face in his hands tenderly, like he's holding an egg.

Evangeline nods. "I know," she says, a little more softly. "But they all came anyway."

She's still very young, and I'm still not so old. There's ash in her hair, and her eyes are bright. I'd rather be afraid of her than for her to be afraid. So I nod.

She leans against me. "I told you it's the witching hour," she murmurs.

I look back at the fire. A corner of the library has collapsed, and smoke pours furiously out of the hole in the building's side. My eyes rove over crumbling joists and tendrils of flame creeping through shattered window frames, and I shake my head a little, trying to sever the connection. It's just a building, they'll make another one, we'll find more books—at least no one is trapped inside.

Still, something is.

Evangeline nudges my hip, but I'm not asleep this time, I'm just watching. The blaze is a piece of our world disappearing, and it's not beautiful, but it's also not unbeautiful. It will never look like this again, and we will never stand together again to watch it go.

My sister is humming a song I recognize but don't quite remember now. But the woman standing next to us does. She hums along with Evangeline, who brightens at the sound. Slowly, a few people behind us pick up the tune, their voices trickling in hesitantly at first, then sweeping into a steady stream.

I turn slowly to look at the crowd behind us. More and more of our bath-robed, bed-headed neighbors join in, their ragged, smoky voices lifting. Emboldened by the choir she inadvertently created, Evangeline sings the loudest, awash in the crest of the chorus, reflecting back the fire's light.

It's not beautiful, but it's not unbeautiful.

If this were a story, we'd sing the last refrain, and some terrible spell would break and the blaze would gutter and extinguish. We would maybe even salvage what's inside, if this were a story.

If this were a story, I would remember the words to the song.

But it's not, and I can't, and the fire keeps casting its resolute sparks against the sky. When the song ends, the resulting quiet burns as fiercely as the flames, and I blink a blur of useless water from my eyes. And we stand there in the silence—shoulder to shoulder, witness to witness—and we watch.

I look down at Evangeline, who, smiling faintly, links her arm with mine. "Good idea, Maya," she tells me.

"What do you mean?" I ask her in a whisper.

"The song," she says.

"That wasn't my idea."

"Yes, it was," she says, wide-eyed. "You asked me if I was singing. When you woke up. You knew."

Then, as though the stories igniting at the edge of the dawn are simply moving on instead of burning out, she tilts her head up to watch the fire again—my sister, who is still, somehow, unafraid.

Whispering Hills
By Jolin Chan

They have tried to cover me up, a shell
of a man speaks to me with a cold, gripping
touch. An unraveling skull of strands eroding
whit by whit. Standing over whispering hills,
antecedents meters below feet—our feet,
and blood on our hands that seep into his
alabaster joints. A literal shell, pale and brittle
and eyes wide open, wound still replaying
and replaying in the back of his head. *Stop,*
rewind, okay, begin. Stop, rewind—
He tells me he's danced with Death,
but it's not as bad as you might think.
The only dread is the frayed black silk
that tickles his toes and the brittle stumbles.
Other than that, bones match bones
and sunken eyes meet sunken eyes
and dust joins dust. *It's more of a mirror*
than a dance. But when you're trapped
between rocks and soil, you make do.
Is it as blue as I remember? A rapt request—
I forget our heads are underground. I say yes,
waving away the fire burning down Maple Street
while gunmetal-gray ashes settle on my soles.
And the green? Have they regrown? It has
overflown so the green is everywhere. A bubbling
influx streaming downward, gathers on its way.
One day, there will be a dance with green
and purple and blue and red, a syrupy red
darker than the ones that have already dried.
And when we waltz down a rebuilt Maple Street,
around the bubbling green, there will be clapping
and tears and shrieks. And the shell of the man
will watch and so will our antecedents.

Vindication
By E.R. Donnelly

My darkest love,

the sliding creek in your voice

as it settles with the afternoon

bronze woven in its parting currents

your hands of packed soil, living green

teased from the roots of your wrists

slender bridges pressing forward

your arms of brass and drums

raising patterned steps against

a brazen ivy chest cracked

open to a wildflower heart

stems locked in the quiet end of day

Here my hands will sleep in yours

and I will wake before you wake

To let night against our long windows.

to follow the gravity of your motion.

Selected Poems by Joanna Acevedo

religion question

my religion is your ribcage.
      i come to your body to worship. at the altar
of your hip bone
      i hang myself. *do you want me*
too? you are a phantom limb
      that still aches.

it is blasphemous
      to want someone this much.
i wait, counting days like two-faced coins.
      someday, possibly soon
you will drip back into my life,
      a leaky faucet of desire run dry
from too much wanting.

you are church, priest, prayer.
      i click rosary beads together
on the face of your photograph. my wrists
      want to be underneath your wrists.
do you want me too?
      you are the pause between hard questions.

Don't Call It A Comeback

I ration myself out like milk in coffee,
A little at a time. A month's budget of sweetness expended
In a tongue's trip, a slip

Of the heart. You are coming back,
October you say. I still remember how I almost loved
Your violence. In that room above the street, on Melrose
Your dog nosed my thighs. I smoked a Marlboro
Into an empty beer can. You explained to me
The blues.

He says he misses me,
In the way it's just a little bit fun
To see how much throttle you're willing to give the car
Once you pull out onto the road.
He says it in a way that makes me think
It's not a compliment.

The chemical taste in the back of my throat
Reminds me of you. In your grip, I am reduced
To my basest desires, a sex object
With arms and legs. I struggle to reclaim my grasp
On needs and wants. When you come back—
What will happen? I'm not sure
I really want to know.

Like a Thief
By Moira Walsh
for W.

Stealing my darkness
the summer comes greedy

Slicing from both
ends of the bread

Lilacs fade
as light takes over

Elderflowers
honey the air

Still I'm too shy to say it
You're wonderful

Selected Poems by Hannah J. Haas

Spine

Tucson stretches houses
       right up to the edge of Sabino Canyon, a crux
in the Santa Catalina Mountains
     where, even in summer, the river runs
         Hiking here with a friend, years ago,
dusk started to fall, and from the trail,
     we could smell the musk of javelinas near us.
We heard coyotes howl in the distance,
         and quickly kept going.

This time, the woman in the gate booth
        gives us a pamphlet on what to do
if we encounter a mountain lion—spread your arms
    to make yourself look bigger,
put something between yourself and the lion
         don't bend down.

We decide to take the loop trail
       that stays in view of the Nature Center
and I picture what we won't see—
    the clutch of trees nestled by the stream,
     the waterfalls, the ridges and rocks beyond us,
but it's June—10:00 a.m., with the temperature
       creeping toward 107 degrees,
and even without the possibility of a lion,
   we aren't acclimated enough to walk much farther.

I know the Sonoran Desert well enough
     to know that I don't know it well enough.
Lightning in the mountains means wildfires.
    Hiking in a box canyon when a storm comes up
means the rescue team will find your bodies

downstream, ground against the rock.
Turning over stones reveals scorpions.

The mountains jag their reliefs in the distance
            and the saguaros, wearing crowns of white flowers
reach their arms up to the wisps of clouds in the sky.
        You spot a white-tailed fawn
gingerly eating leaves
                    from the range ratany and fairy duster.
Volunteers in the nature center told us
        they'd heard that flooding
                    had changed the pools in the watershed
driving the deer and the lions down farther.
            A quail family runs from bush to bush for cover.
    A rabbit statues itself before a barrel cactus.
                        A lizard skitters away.

Once, in spring, a friend took me up to Redington Pass
        where a trail crosses through the stream
                and after months without rain, I was wading
through pools of cool water
        surrounded by boulders and cliffs
pines in the distance, and people sunning themselves
                        on the tiny, silt beaches.
I stopped on the trail to look up at the sky,
                        and on the ridge above us
was a man wearing only hiking boots—
        nothing to put between himself and a lion,
almost nothing between his skin and the spikes and spines.

Attraction

I grazed Tombstone with a friend stopping for gas.
             Peering down the dirt streets in passing,
we were surprised by the cowboy in spurs
             leaning against the saloon, by the costumed
Can-can dancer—the whole town a celebration
                   of the gunfight at the OK Corral,
        which didn't actually take place there.

Twenty-four percent of Arizonans
      have never visited the Grand Canyon, yet have suffered
             a lifetime of postcards and magnets.
Later, I'd edit tourism magazines,
      I'd work with a woman who'd been a Tombstone actor.
She'd laugh about it, and no one would ask
             whether she'd been wife or madam,
                         barmaid or dancer.
The landscape was our small city's real attraction,
        and the readers stayed at resorts
                   in the bulldozed foothills
surrounded by manicured greens.

Downtown was a strange collision
                   of transplants from around the country.
While so many Midwesterners have Grand Canyon
      family misadventure stories,
   the few Arizonans I knew skipped the state's destinations,
        told stories of their parents' summer strategies
for making the six-hour trip to San Diego without
        passing through Yuma at noon
                   when the temperature tops 115 degrees,
of the holidays they'd spent in the E.R.
      waiting for a relative to have cactus spines removed—

touch football and four wheeler casualties—
of the lengths their parents would go to
to get the best masa for Christmas tamales.

I went to the Grand Canyon the week I first arrived,
stood at the rim
and found it unfathomable.
We travel out and return, see or don't see
all the way down to the final sedimentary layer.
The simple fact of the masses of bodies
pulls them toward one another.

Milagros

I waited inside San Miguel, the oldest church,
to ring the bell that some say hung in Spain
and then Mexico. It came to Santa Fe by oxcart

for the bell tower, and is suspended now
from a wooden frame at the back of the church,
whose thick adobe walls look like they were hewn from rock.

My turn came, and I took up the rubber mallet
and tapped the bell. A dull tone rang over the pews—
I hadn't swung hard enough at history.

The thick frame the bell hangs from is covered in silver milagros—
arms and legs, horses, kneeling men in prayer—
symbols of miracles asked for, and thanks for hundreds

of wounds already healed. It sits on the hardwood floor
rebuilt over original planks so old they've almost
been worn into the dirt where priests are buried

within the church walls. I supposed they knew
that they would rest under the creaking of our footsteps
as we looked at the saints carved into the reredos,

that there would be floorboards above them rather
than the maniacal radiance of the New Mexican sky.
I thought of the medals of Saints my mother

told me my grandmother pinned to her bras.
I wasn't even baptized, but if I'd had in my pocket,
a silver boy, a silver girl, would the caretakers have let me

fix my hopes for them to the frame?
Could my grandmother's Saints, the bell, the priests' bones
have kept the illnesses we didn't know were coming
at bay long enough to usher our children to us?

The Surest Sign of Fire
By Eli Slover

The black smoke rises
over trees born in the last century.
The old forest is burning again.
The great forests must burn
in these moonless nights,
else stagnation alone grows.
Reincarnation is liminal
and renaissance is uncertain
at this point. The fullness of
night is unabridged by
moon or star
which is why
the fire seems so fierce.
The fire is fierce.
It must be.
Flames must be destructive
and ruthless
and consuming,
else some bitter plant,
some vessel of old life,
a relic of the dying forest
might yet survive
and destroy the work
of the new generation,
because the forest doesn't listen
to anything but violence--
at least, not yet.

The Shopping List
By Ashley Bray

Thanksgiving break was nine days, 216 hours, and 12,960 minutes long. I'd only managed to pass 10 of those minutes FaceTiming with my girlfriend in the parking lot of my parents' temporary apartment outside of Boston.

"Are you gonna go in?" she asked, the screen bobbing as she walked down a flight of stairs.

"Eventually."

"What are you worried about?"

I stared out at the blocky, tan apartment building so I didn't have to look at Zoey. It had been almost two months since I'd last seen Dad before leaving for my senior year of boarding school. He was going to look different. He always did. And how he'd changed was enough to tell me whether or not a particular treatment was working. "I don't know. I guess I'm just being stupid."

"Chris, look at me."

I did.

"It's OK to be worried about him. It's not stupid."

We'd only been dating a few months, but already it felt like she knew me in a deeper way than I'd intended—like I'd left a forgotten window open to my most secret thoughts.

An artificial light bathed her face in white. "You can't

spend the entire break in your truck. Go in."

"What are you doing?"

"Trying to find something to eat in this place that isn't granola or kale. My parents are on a health kick." She flipped the camera so that I could see the inside of the fridge she was searching. "Can you identify any of this crap? I'm gonna go get a double cheeseburger and eat it in front of them."

"I think I see some pickles back there."

She flipped back to the front-facing camera and raised an eyebrow. "Pickles? Think of me this week when you're eating whatever delicious carb-filled Italian feasts your mom's making."

It was like Zoey had spoken her into being; she was rushing down the front steps of the apartment building. "Chris!" she exclaimed.

"My mom saw me. Gotta go."

"All right. Call me later."

I hung up and got out of the truck.

Mom pulled me into a hug, which required me to basically fold in half. "We missed you! C'mon in, Dad can't wait to see you." She opened the door to the backseat and reached for my bag.

"Mom, that weighs more than you. I got it," I said pulling her away from the door. I hoisted the bag over my shoulder and followed her inside.

My parents had temporarily relocated from Jersey to Boston so that Dad could participate in an experimental drug trial—the last rung on a ladder he'd been steadily descending for the last two years. The apartment was an unfamiliar place, but it still smelled like home—antiseptic laced with Mom's perfume and the lavender candles she always burned, plus the hint of…tomato sauce.

I dropped my bag beside the recliner. "You made gravy?"

"Of course! It's your homecoming gift," she said, rubbing my arm.

I followed her into the kitchen and made a beeline for the big pot with red sauce simmering on the stove, but Dad caught my arm in his bony fingers. His grip was still surprisingly strong.

"Didn't see you," I said, backtracking and sitting in the chair across from him at the round kitchen table. We weren't the hugging type. "How are you feeling?"

"Like I might run the New York Marathon this year," he cracked.

The skin hung looser around his neck than it had in September—like he didn't even fit in his own body anymore. The knuckles of his hands were knobby and protruding as he swept the cards from his solitaire game into a pile.

But maybe he'd always been that thin, and I'd just forgotten.

I grabbed the cards, shuffled them, and dealt out two hands for gin rummy.

"So Chris, we're going to have to make do for the week," Mom said as she stirred the sauce. "We got the apartment furnished, but there's only one bedroom. The couch opens up into a bed though, so we're going to put you there, if that's OK."

"Can't be worse than the beds at school," I said, pulling out a sequence of three cards.

"You get that Rensselaer college app in?" Dad asked, picking up the top card from the discard pile.

I nodded. "Portfolio for the architecture program and all."

"What'd you put in the portfolio?"

"I'll show you." I put my cards face-down on the table and pulled my phone out.

Dad tried to sneak a peek at my cards. I slapped my hand down on them and scrolled through the files on my phone with my other hand. "Don't cheat just because you can't win against me anymore."

"I taught you everything you know."

I handed my phone to him. "Scroll down and you'll see all the sketches."

He was quiet for a while as he scrolled through the PDF. "You and these damn houses. You ever think of designing a commercial building?"

"That's your contractor talking."

"There's more money in commercial buildings."

"I haven't even gotten in yet. I'll have plenty of time to design a boring office building."

He squinted and brought the phone closer. A grin stretched the skin tight across his face. I knew just the sketch he'd come across—the one I'd forgotten about when I handed my phone to him. "That your girl?" he asked, turning the phone around to show me the sketch of Zoey, her head tilted to one side so that her hair cascaded over one shoulder, a half smile on her face, with the New York by Gehry skyscraper rippling up behind her.

I grabbed for the phone, but he pulled it back, laughing in his raspy way.

"Let me see," Mom said, turning from the salad she was putting together. She leaned over Dad's shoulder to get a look. "Do you have an actual picture of her?"

"Yeah, let's see if this drawing holds up," Dad said as he handed the phone back to me, "or if infatuation is blinding."

"Well, this is awkward," I said, scrolling through my photos to find a good one of Zoey. I chose a selfie I'd taken of us on my birthday.

Dad let out a low whistle. "How'd you snag her?"

Mom smacked his arm. "Anthony! Have some faith in your son."

I laughed. We might have been in a strange place, and Dad might have looked different, but all of this still felt like *before*—when drugs full of consonants and oxygen tanks with miles of tubing that always tangled weren't a part of our lives.

Dad pushed up from the table, the motion taking more effort than it used to. "I'll be right back."

"Where you going, Ant?" Mom asked, hovering.

"Can a man take a leak without being interrogated?"

Mom threw her hands up. "Fine, fine."

Dad shuffled over to the door that led back into the carpeted living room. One minute he was standing and the next he was on the ground, the oxygen tank falling over next to him like it couldn't stand to be away from him for even a moment.

I jumped up, suddenly breathless myself, and beat Mom to the door. "Jesus, Dad! You all right?"

I grabbed him under the arms and lifted him to his

feet—more easily than I had anticipated. Dad had towered over me until a few years ago. He'd always been this strong, treelike presence that lifted up cinderblocks at job sites like they were made of Styrofoam.

Mom righted the oxygen tank, and together we helped him to the recliner in the living room.

My ears were hot with secondhand embarrassment. He'd never fallen before. It was like my mind couldn't compute having seen him splayed out on the floor—helpless.

I reached to right the crooked cannula that had become dislodged from one side of his nose.

He pushed my hand away, and I stepped back as he fixed it himself. He looked more like Dad with the cannula in. It had become another part of his face, like a freckle or a crooked nose.

"Damn bag!" he said, trying to catch his breath.

"What?" Mom asked.

"The bag!" he shouted, gesturing to the duffel bag I'd left beside the recliner.

"Dad, my bag was nowhere near the door."

"I was trying to avoid it," he said, breathing normal now that the oxygen was flowing again. "I tripped!"

I looked to Mom.

"We'll move it, Ant. Don't worry about it." She reached

down and strained to lift the bag before I could stop her.

"Are you gonna let your mother carry that thing?"

I took the bag from her. It was like he'd done a complete 180 in eight seconds.

"And don't leave your shit lying around! I'm not gonna have this place look like the inside of your Goddamn bedroom."

"Anthony, c'mon—"

"I don't even have a room. So where the hell am I supposed to put everything?" I dropped the bag.

He shook his head. Just get out of my sight," he said, waving his hand dismissively at me.

"Really, Dad? Should I just go back to school now? Because I've been here for like ten minutes, and I'm already done."

He pointed at me. "Listen, smartass—"

Mom stepped in front of me. "Chris, go stir the sauce."

I stepped around her, but she grabbed my arm. "Christopher. The kitchen. Now."

I rolled my eyes but went back to the kitchen. I grabbed the wooden spoon and stirred the sauce until it was just a red whirlpool below me. They were whispering in the other room like I was a little kid. Next, they'd start spelling words they didn't want me to hear.

Mom appeared beside me and put her hand over mine. I let her take the spoon. "He's not mad at you."

"Could have fooled me."

"Chris, please."

I crossed my arms over my chest. "Then who's he really mad at, Mom?"

"Himself," she snapped. "He doesn't like to admit that he can't do the things he used to be able to do because of…it. Little things. Like leaving a damn room."

We always said "it," like we were afraid that naming it would give it extra power.

The tiny lines around Mom's mouth deepened as she frowned at me. "Try to understand that. OK?"

What I couldn't understand was why that made it OK for him to take it all out on me. I wasn't going to spend this week being the scapegoat for all of Dad's insecurities.

I fell back into the chair at the kitchen table. All at once, everything felt like *after* again, and the familiar tangle of nerves wound tighter together in my stomach.

Mom steadied herself against the counter. "This lung cancer drug is going to be the one that works," she said, nodding.

She had named it.

My skin itched—like there wasn't enough space inside

of myself.

She was still nodding, her knuckles white around the handle of the wooden spoon.

I stood up. I had to get out of here. "I'll be back."

Mom turned. "What? Where are you going?"

I didn't respond. I'd forgotten my winter coat, so I plucked Dad's wool overcoat from the hook by the door along with my bag—maybe I wouldn't come back at all.

I drove the few minutes into Boston and parked on the outskirts where I could still find a space without much trouble. I pulled my sketchbook and a pencil out of my bag and walked the rest of the way.

I found a bench in the park across from the State House and started to sketch the building. The proportions and ratios, the way the angles and curves fit together, the placement of windows and doors—it all had an order and a purpose. It all made sense.

There weren't many people in the park, it was freezing, but the few who were here didn't pay me any attention. It was nice to lose myself in the anonymity of a big city again. I missed New York in a way I never had before because it had always been right there—glinting across the Hudson River in vertical rows of lights.

I finished the sketch and pulled my phone out to

FaceTime with Zoey, but she didn't answer. The wind slipped under the collar of Dad's coat. I flipped it up, but that made things worse because then the woodsy scent of his cologne filled my nose.

I shoved my hands into the pockets of the coat. My numb fingers hit a piece of paper. It was a CVS receipt. I almost crumpled it up but stopped when I saw Dad's neat, all-capitals handwriting on the back. All those years of reading blueprints had molded his handwriting, and I'd picked it up from him.

He'd written: *WATER, TOOTHPASTE, COUGH DROPS, CHRIS BDAY CARD*

It was just a shopping list, but there was still a lump in my throat as I stared at my name in his handwriting. Like he was gone or something. Which he wasn't. Not yet.

The dark pressed in around me. The wind blew again, and I felt the time in it rushing past me—like a subway car blowing through a station.

I shoved the receipt back into the coat pocket, grabbed my sketchbook, and ran to the truck. If I hurried, I could make it back to the house in time for a family dinner, which seemed like the most important thing in the world right now.

Contributors:

Cover Artist:

Emily Rankin was born in Riverside, California and attended university in Abilene, TX, where she received a BFA in 2011. Her body of work ranges from Graphic Design to collaborative performances with Verstehen, an improvisational series which incorporates live painting and sound. She is currently based in New Mexico. www.eerankinart.com

Inspiration for *The End of the World #779*

The End of the World #779, Mixed Media on Canvas. This piece makes up a part of an ongoing series of Dream Paintings which seeks to capture the inexpressible feelings and the unreal architecture of dreaming. I'm fascinated by the stories the mind tells itself through dreams and the metaphors which help us to better understand our own consciousness.

Joanna Acevedo is the author of the poetry collection *The Pathophysiology of Longing* (Black Centipede Press, 2020) and the short story collection *Unsaid Things* (Flexible Press, forthcoming 2021). She is a Hospitalfield 2020 Interdisciplinary Resident, NYU Goldwater Fellow, and Prose Editor at *Inklette Magazine*. She is currently an MFA candidate at NYU. Find Joanna on Twitter: @jo_avocado and IG: @joavocado.

Kate Autio is a poet who lives near the frozen shores of Lake Superior. She has a bachelor's degree in English/Creative Writing from Northern Michigan University. In addition to poetry, she also writes flash fiction and short horror screenplays. When she isn't writing, she enjoys playing music for the reluctant audience of her cat.

Ashley Bray holds a B.A. in English from Fordham University and is the editor-in-chief of a trade magazine. She lives in Rhode Island with her partner and dog. When she's not writing, you can find her binging true crime documentaries and podcasts. Follow her on Twitter: @ashleymbray.

Despy Boutris is a writer. Her work is published or forthcoming in *American Poetry Review*, *Southern Indiana Review*, *Copper Nickel*, *Colorado Review*, *The Adroit Journal*, *Prairie Schooner*, *Palette Poetry*, *Raleigh Review*, and elsewhere. Currently, she teaches at the University of Houston, serves as Editor-in-Chief for *The West Review*, and works as an Assistant Poetry Editor at *Gulf Coast*.

Jolin Chan is a Chinese American writer and student living in Irvine, California. She has been recognized by the International Kusamakura Haiku Competition, the Scholastic Art and Writing Awards, Princeton University, the YoungArts Foundation, and more. Her work has been published or is forthcoming in Westwind, Frogpond Journal, and the New Zealand Poetry Society's anthology. Find Jolin on Instagram: @jolin.c.

Marisa P. Clark is a queer writer from the South whose work appears or will appear in *Shenandoah, Cream City Review, Nimrod, Epiphany, Crab Creek Review, Foglifter, Potomac Review, Rust + Moth, Jabberwock Review, Indianapolis Review, Folio,* and elsewhere. *Best American Essays 2011* recognized her writing among its Notable Essays. A fiction reader for *New England Review,* she makes her home in New Mexico with three parrots and two dogs. Her first name is pronounced Ma-REE-sa.

Renea Di Bella (she/they) is a queer, gender fluid, poet, blogger, and suicide survivor. She has a B.A. in Secondary

Education and an M.A. in Curriculum and Instruction. Renea was born and raised in Michigan, spending a middle-class upbringing as an over-achieving type-A perfectionist and budding workaholic. Renea spent five years teaching middle school. Then, after experiencing burnout during the typical fifth year of teaching, she suffered a breakdown that changed everything. Renea's poetry is a reflection of her lifelong journeys with mental illness, sexuality, gender, and identity. You can find Renea's poetry on both Twitter and Instagram at @_r_d_b__.

E.R. Donnelly's work has appeared or is forthcoming in the *Tulane Review*, *Santa Ana River Review*, and *Great Lakes Review*. Originally from the midwest, she now resides on the East Coast with family.

Jamie A. Grove's work has been featured in 805 Lit+Art, Parentheses Journal, Abstract Magazine, as well as other literary journals and has been nominated for the Best of the Net. She lives on the dry side of Oregon, with her family, where she spends most of her free time haunting the library, hiking, and gardening. Find Jamie on Instagram: @j.a.grove.

Hannah J. Haas received her M.F.A. in creative writing from the University of Arizona. She is a member of the English faculty at Indiana University-Purdue University Indianapolis. Her work has appeared in journals such as *ACM, Folio,* and *Inscape.*

Courtney Harler is a freelance writer, editor, and educator based in Las Vegas, Nevada. She holds an MFA from Sierra Nevada University (2017) and an MA from Eastern Washington University (2013). Courtney has been honored by fellowships from Writing By Writers, Squaw Valley Community of Writers, and Nevada Arts Council. Courtney's written work—which includes poems, flash fictions, short stories, literary analyses, craft essays, book and film reviews, author interviews, personal essays, and hybrid pieces—has been published worldwide. Links to her publications and other related awards can be found at https://harlerliterary.llc. Find her on Twitter: @CourtneyHarler1 and Instagram: @CourtneyHarler.

Sarah Jane Justice writes lyrical poetry, whimsical character pieces, and thrilling genre fiction. Her poetry has been featured in releases from *The Blue Nib*, *Capsule Stories*, and *Pure Slush*, and her short fiction has been published by The *Bombay Review*, *Caustic Frolic*, and *Adelaide Literary Magazine*. In addition to the written word, she is a celebrated spoken word artist, having won an array of competition titles and performed at the Sydney Opera House. Find Sarah on IG: @sarahjanejusticewriting and Twitter: @sjjusticewrites.

Rimsha Kashif is a medical student at Midwestern University. Her roots are embedded in Pakistan but her adolescence was spent in the United States. Born in 1997, she is a contemporary artist who uses her work to document narratives of adversity, growth, and healing. Rimsha has been published by the *Kettle Blue Review* for her work: "The 'What I Should Have Said' Dictionary." Find her on Instagram at: @rimshakashif_.

DS Maolalai has been nominated eight times for Best of the Net and five times for the Pushcart Prize. His poetry has been released in two collections, *Love is Breaking Plates in the Garden* (Encircle Press, 2016) and *Sad Havoc Among the Birds* (Turas Press, 2019).

Alan Meyrowitz retired in 2005 after a career in computer research. His writing has appeared in *Dark Ink Anthology*, *Eclectica*, *Esthetic Apostle*, *Existere*, *From Whispers to Roars*, *Inwood Indiana*, *Jitter*, *The Literary Hatchet*, *The Nassau*

Review, *Poetry Quarterly*, *Schuylkill Valley Journal*, *Shark Reef*, *Shroud*, *Spirit's Tincture*, and others.

Nell Ovitt is a writer and artist from North Carolina. Her writing has appeared in *Okay Donkey Magazine* and *The Sunlight Press*, and her short script was a semifinalist in the 2020 Atlanta Film Festival Screenplay contest. She works in storytelling in many forms, including theatre, film, and radio. Lately, she's been relearning how to play piano, making lots of coffee, waving at dogs, and keeping an eye out for signs of spring. Find her on Instagram/Twitter: @nellcyrene.

Kim Jay Rose grew up in a London suburb, influenced by a traditional British education heavy on literature and language, as well as by her parents' diverse musical tastes. She lives in Gainesville, Florida, works in strategic communications and sometimes sings in a band. Her poems have appeared in print and online at *Bacopa Literary Review*, Burrow Press, and the *Pittsburgh Poetry Journal*. She's on Twitter @KimJayRose.

Kaitlyn San Miguel is a queer Filipina-American writer based in Princeton, New Jersey. She works in the proofreading department of HarperCollins Publishers, moonlights as a liberal arts graduate student at Johns Hopkins University, and reviews books by BIPOC writers on her Instagram, @decolonizedbookcase. Her poetry has been published in *Cosmonauts Avenue* and *petrichor*. This is her first short story publication.

Nancy Sarafian holds an MFA, Writing from the University of San Francisco. Her work has appeared in *The Armenian Weekly*. The themes of her writing show her broad interests from feminism and politics to the environment and sports. It is a vocation that continues to both excite and challenge her.

Eli Slover is a poet and student at university studying creative writing. His work in poetry has been seen in Go Anywhere, Page & Spine, Yes Poetry, and elsewhere. He serves as an assistant poetry editor for *Moon City Review*. Find Eli on Twitter: @slover_eli.

Frankie A Soto is a 2x winner of the Multicultural Poet of the year award from the National Spoken Word Poetry Awards in Chicago. His (*New York Times*) performance called him an absolute force. He's been featured on ABC news and has traveled all across the country featuring at over 130 Universities & Colleges actively touring/performing and running workshops. He's been published worldwide for online and print publications. Find Frankie on IG: @Frankiesotopoetry or on Twitter: @Frankiesotopoet.

Dorsía Smith Silva is a Pushcart Prize nominee, Obsidian Fellow, and Professor of English at the University of Puerto Rico, Río Piedras. Her poetry has been published or is forthcoming in *Superstition Review*, *Porter House Review*, *Portland Review*, *Pidgeonholes*, *SAND*, and elsewhere. She is also the author of Good Girl (micro-chapbook), editor of Latina/Chicana Mothering, and the co-editor of six books. She has a Ph.D. in Caribbean Literature and Language. Her website is dorsiasmithsilva.com.

Sophia Thimmes has been published in *The Ekphrastic Review* and *Sink Hollow,* and has presented on spoken word poetry at national conferences. She can often be found hiking in the woods, munching on carb-based foods, and becoming overly enthused about fat snowflakes falling in Utah, where she studies creative writing at Utah State University and works as an English tutor.

Upasana writes fiction and poetry to makes sense of the world. Originally from India, she currently lives in the SF Bay

Area where she works in tech for a living, and eats books and stories for breakfast, lunch and dinner. Find her on IG: @upasanadatta.

Michigan-born **Moira Walsh** has lived on three continents and is currently based in Germany, where she writes and translates. She became a published poet in 2020. Moira is the 2021 Anne-Marie Oomen Fellow at Poetry Forge and was a Thomas Lux Scholar at the 2021 Palm Beach Poetry Festival. https://linktr.ee/moira_walsh. Find Moira on IG: @poetbynecessity.

Lilian Caylee Wang won a writing contest as a five-year-old in Tennessee. Since then, she's eaten countless PB&J sandwiches, created an anthology of the lives of San Francisco's homeless, fallen in love with people and places, written essays about culture and food, and become a poet. Her work has been published in the Huffington Post, Whetstone Magazine, The Racket, sPARKLE & bLINK, and more. Currently, she works as a product designer and lives on the road with her partner and her puppy. Find Lillian on Twitter: liliancaylee and Instagram: @lilreadsandwrites/@liliancaylee.

Ayanna Wimberly is a screen, play, and creative writer and graduate of NYU Tisch School of the Arts. She's fresh off the heels of her first publication, a chapbook full of sometimes quippy always shoegazing poetry, *Like A Fire*, through Finishing Line Press. She currently lives and writes in Chicago.

Maggie Wolff is a queer writer of poetry, fiction, and creative nonfiction. Her work appears in *The Lascaux Review*, *Saw Palm*, *34th Parallel Magazine*, and *Qu Literary Magazine*. She is working on her first poetry collection, which follows three generations of women as they navigate depression, addiction, and suicide. She's a poetry candidate in the MFA creative writing program at the University of Central Florida. She lives in Orlando, FL with her wife, two dogs, and a very vocal cat.

Thank you for reading! Stay in touch:

www.blackfoxlitmag.com
Website

www.facebook.com/blackfoxlit
Facebook

@blackfoxlit
Twitter & Instagram

www.blackfoxlitmag.com/contact/
Newsletter

Check out some of our previous issues:

Find more of our issues at blackfoxlitmag.com!

Resources for Writers from BFLM Editor Racquel Henry's Writer's Atelier:

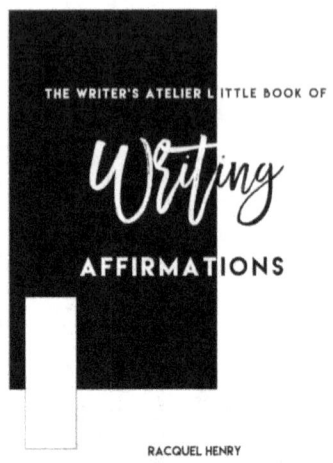

The Writer's Atelier Little Book of Writing Affirmations

The Complete Revision Workbook for Writers